To Sara and Hana Cepić
And love to Monika and Luka, my two big bouncers.

WWW.DAVIDMELLING.CO.UK

We Love You, Hugless Douglas!

BY David Melling

It was a bright and beautiful kind of a day.

A *day for sharing with friends*, thought Douglas. So he went out to look for someone to play with.

Only he couldn't find anyone.

Anywhere.

Until he heard a noise…

"Hello, Flossie," said Douglas. "How did you get up there?"

Flossie took a deep breath.
"I was playing hide-and-seek with
**MY BEST FRIEND
LITTLE SHEEP** and I got
stuck and now he's lost and…."

"Don't worry," said Douglas.
And he placed Flossie gently
on the ground.

Flossie gave Douglas a **THANK YOU HUG**.

"Will you please help me find Little Sheep?"
she sniffed.

"Of course I will," said Douglas.

And together they headed off to do just that.

They soon passed the Old Barn and found Cow and her best friend preparing milkshakes for everyone.

"Hellooo!" said Cow. "Take a seat, and we'll make you strawberry and banana smooooooo-thies!"

"We can't stop now, Cow," said Douglas. "We're looking for Little Sheep. Have you seen him?"

Cow looked under the table. "Nooooo!" she said. "Have you tried going down, through, and around?"

Douglas wasn't quite sure what she meant but thanked her all the same and hurried on.

Douglas and Flossie made their way down the hill, through the long, tickly grass toward Tall Tree Wood.

They were busy searching around when all of a sudden, they were surprised by three flying bunnies!

"Good catch!" said Rabbit. "Have you come to join our class, **BEST FRIEND BOUNCERS?**"

"No," said Douglas. "We're looking for Little Sheep."

"Too bad. I could do with a catcher for my big bouncers," Rabbit sighed. "Well, if you're looking for sheep, why don't you try Baa Baa Bush?"

By the time they reached Baa Baa Bush,
Flossie was very excited.

"Let's see what we can find in here," said Douglas,
and he rummaged around in the leaves.

There was no sign of any sheep. But Flossie wriggled
and squeaked and asked Douglas to look again....

"Found you, Little Sheep!"
cried Flossie.

"BEST FRIENDS TOGETHER AT LAST,"
smiled Douglas.

The two sheep looked so happy and trotted off hand in hand.

Douglas waved good-bye to them. **"I WISH *I* HAD A BEST FRIEND,"** he said.

Close by,
wise old Owl
heard his wish.

Douglas wondered why he felt so sad and sat down to think for a while.

He was just about to head home when he heard
a rustling sound behind him....

Everyone was there!

"We heard you needed a best friend," said Rabbit.
"So we all came to find you."

Douglas realized how silly he had been.
"Of course! We're *all* best friends together."

"We love you, Hugless Douglas!" everyone cried.

"AND I LOVE YOU, TOO,"
smiled Douglas.

I ♥ pins

We ♥ piggyback
rides

I ♥ muddy puddle

I ♥ drawing

I ♥ ladybugs

I ♥ my mom

We ♥ bouncing

I ♥ my best friend

I ♥ pudding

I ♥ books

I ♥ my dad

tiger tales
5 River Road, Suite 128, Wilton, CT 06897
Published in the United States 2014
Originally published in Great Britain 2013
by Hodder Children's Books
a division of Hachette Children's Books
Text and illustrations copyright © 2013 David Melling
www.huglessdouglas.co.uk
Wkt0612
ISBN-13: 978-1-58925-138-0
ISBN-10: 1-58925-138-5
Printed in China
All rights reserved
10 9 8 7 6 5 4 3 2 1

For more insight and activities,
visit us at www.tigertalesbooks.com